W9-DAV-124

HELLO KITTY®

Presents the
Fairytale Collection

HELLO KITTY®

Presents the
Fairytale Collection

Abrams Books for Young Readers

New York

LIVINGSTON PUBLIC LIBRARY
10 Robert Harp Drive
Livingston, NJ 07039

Contents

Alice's Adventures in Wonderland 1

Thumbelina 33

Little Red Riding Hood 65

The Little Mermaid 97

The Nutcracker & The Mouse King 129

HELLO KITTY®

Alice's Adventures in Wonderland

On a beautiful summer day, Hello Kitty
and her sister, Mimmy, had a picnic.
After they ate, Mimmy read a book while
Hello Kitty lazily counted clouds.

Suddenly, a squirrel ran by.

4

"Oh dear," he cried. "I'm late! I'm late!"
As Hello Kitty watched, the squirrel disappeared
into a nearby hedge. Curious, Hello Kitty followed.

Down, down, down

she fell, leaving Mimmy and their picnic behind.

6

When she reached the bottom, Hello Kitty saw
the squirrel dash through a tiny door. Hello Kitty
wanted to follow, but she was far too big.

Hello Kitty looked around the room. On a table nearby, she spotted a golden key and a small bottle. Attached to the bottle was a card that read, "Drink me."

10 Hello Kitty took a drink. At first nothing happened.
Then she felt herself get smaller and smaller!

Finally, she was small
enough to fit through the tiny
door. She unlocked it with
the key and dashed through,
looking for the squirrel.

On the other side of the door was a beautiful garden.
Hello Kitty took a moment to enjoy the flowers.

In the garden, Hello Kitty found a large
mushroom. There was a caterpillar sitting on top.
"Are you looking for that little squirrel?"
the caterpillar asked. Hello Kitty nodded.

"I think he went that way," the caterpillar said.
Hello Kitty thanked the caterpillar and went on her way.

15

When Hello Kitty found the squirrel, he was enjoying afternoon tea. Finally, Hello Kitty understood. The squirrel had been late for a tea party!

Hello Kitty had a sip of tea and a bite of cake with the squirrel, the Mad Hatter, and the Dormouse. But she was eager to explore, so she thanked them and was on her way.

She came upon three gardeners dressed like
cards. They seemed very worried and very busy.
They had planted white roses, but the Queen of
Hearts only liked red. So the gardeners were
very busy painting the white roses red.

20

And they were very worried that the
Queen of Hearts would notice and be upset.

It wasn't long before Hello Kitty came across
the Queen of Hearts herself. She was happily

playing croquet in a garden of red roses.

She was in such a good mood that she invited
Hello Kitty to the castle for tea and tarts.

When they got to the castle, the tarts were gone!
Someone had stolen them!

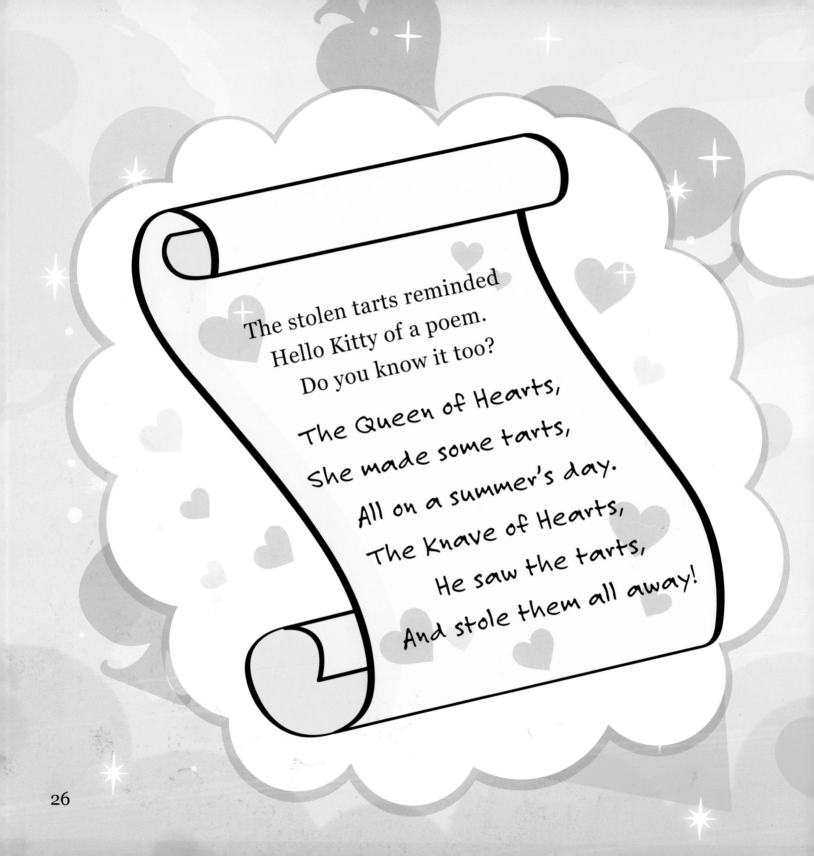

The stolen tarts reminded
Hello Kitty of a poem.
Do you know it too?

The Queen of Hearts,
She made some tarts,
All on a summer's day.
The Knave of Hearts,
He saw the tarts,
And stole them all away!

The Knave of Hearts! Hello Kitty had solved the mystery!
Everyone clapped and cheered.

29

Suddenly, Hello Kitty woke up.
She was back at the picnic with Mimmy.
And she was craving tea and tarts.

HELLO KITTY®
Thumbelina

One afternoon,
a handsome prince invited
Hello Kitty to a dance.

Mama made her a special dress.
Hello Kitty couldn't wait to wear it!

The night before the dance, Hello Kitty
was so excited. When she finally drifted off
to sleep, she had the strangest dream.

37

In Hello Kitty's dream, Mama was a gardener.
In her garden, a magic flower grew.

If Mama took good care of the
flower, it would give her a little girl.
Mama wanted a little girl more
than anything in the world.

One day, the magic flower opened! Inside was
a tiny girl, no bigger than Mama's thumb.

Mama was delighted. She named the little girl
Thumbelina. She gave Thumbelina a walnut shell to sleep
in and a large bowl of water to keep her entertained.

41

During the day, Thumbelina rowed across the water on a tulip petal.
In the evening, she sat at the edge of the bowl and sang.

One evening, a toad heard Thumbelina sing. Enchanted, he
carried her away, thinking she would make a good wife for his son.
He kept Thumbelina on a lily pad in the middle of a pond.

The fish in the pond felt sorry for her.
They chewed the stem of the lily pad
until it broke free and floated away.

44

Thumbelina spent the summer
months alone, singing with the birds.
She ate nectar from the flowers
and drank dew from the grass.

When it grew cold, a mouse and mole invited
Thumbelina to stay in their warm underground home.

One night, as Thumbelina and her friends prepared
for bed, a wounded bird landed in their burrow.

Thumbelina fetched a blanket for the bird and stayed
with him all night. In the morning, the bird felt a bit better.

Days passed. Thumbelina sang to the bird, and he grew stronger and stronger.

Soon, the weather was warm again. Thumbelina
and the bird missed being outside in the sun.

Thumbelina was sad to leave the mouse
and the mole, but it was time to go.

The bird flew and flew, until finally
Thumbelina was back in her village!

The bird landed in a nest that just happened
to be right above where the prince was standing!

Hello Kitty woke with a start.
It was the day of the dance!

Everyone in the village came to the dance dressed in their finest clothes. Hello Kitty wore the dress Mama made for her.

Finally, Hello Kitty danced with the prince!

It was better than a dream come true.

HELLO KITTY®
Little Red Riding Hood

Once upon a time, in a village near the woods, there lived a little girl. Because she always wore a red cape her grandma made for her, everyone called her Little Red Riding Hood.

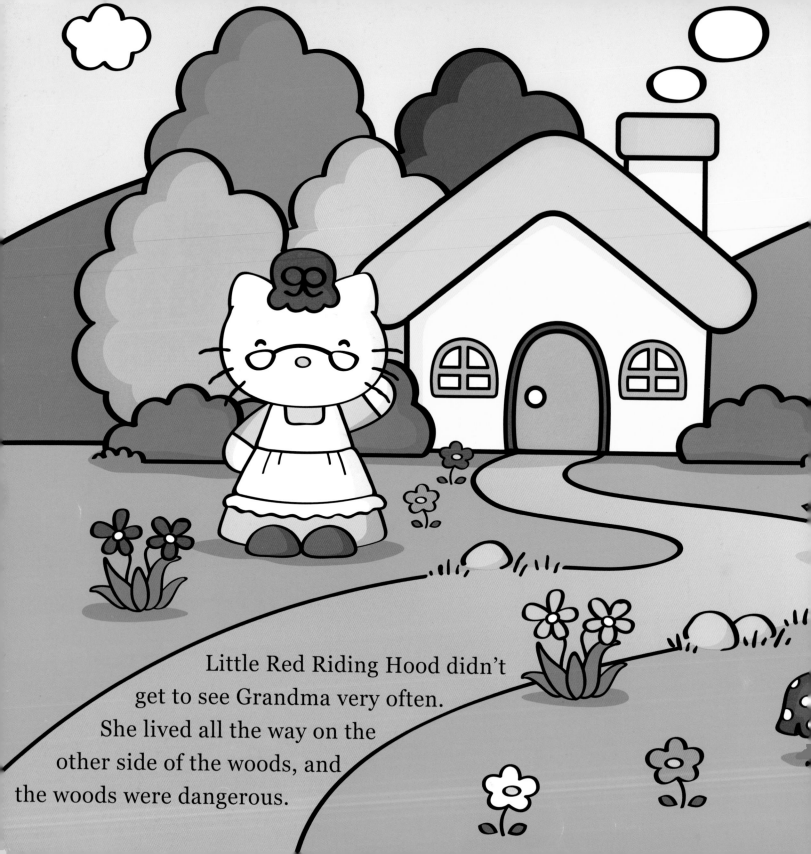

Little Red Riding Hood didn't
get to see Grandma very often.
She lived all the way on the
other side of the woods, and
the woods were dangerous.

But when Little Red Riding Hood learned
Grandma was sick, she decided to be very brave
and pay Grandma a visit.

Mama packed Little Red Riding Hood
a basket full of cookies, soup, and
other treats to take to Grandma.

70

Then she tightened Little Red Riding Hood's cape, kissed her good-bye, and reminded her not to talk to strangers in the woods.

The woods were so lovely and green! Little Red Riding
Hood was enjoying her walk, when suddenly, a wolf
popped out from the bushes!

Little Red Riding Hood was startled, but the wolf
assured her that he just wanted to keep her company
as she walked to Grandma's house.

In the middle of the woods, Little Red Riding Hood
saw a grove of beautiful flowers growing beside a tall tree.
What a nice present they'd make for Grandma!

While Little Red Riding Hood picked the flowers, the wolf scurried away to Grandma's house. Grandma heard the wolf coming and hid in her closet just as the wolf burst through her door.

Thinking Grandma wasn't home,
the wolf decided to play a trick on Little Red
Riding Hood. He put on Grandma's
nightgown and glasses. He got into Grandma's
bed and pulled the covers up to his fuzzy chin.

When Little Red Riding Hood arrived at Grandma's house, she ran to Grandma's bedside. Even though it had been a long time since Little Red Riding Hood had seen her grandma, something seemed different about her.

84

Grandma had such big eyes! All the better to see her with, Little Red Riding Hood supposed. And such big hands! Which, Little Red Riding Hood thought, were probably good for hugging.

But Grandma's mouth! Grandma's mouth seemed the strangest of all! Those teeth looked like they would gobble Little Red Riding Hood right up!

87

Suddenly, the wolf jumped out of the bed, snapping those big teeth at Little Red Riding Hood! That's what was different about Grandma! She wasn't Grandma at all!

Just then, a farmer walking by Grandma's house heard all the commotion. He rushed in and captured the wolf in a net, keeping everyone safe from harm.

90

Grandma popped out of the closet and thanked the farmer.
Feeling much better, she scolded the wolf.

Grandma put the treats Little Red Riding Hood
brought on the table. The farmer, Grandma, and Little
Red Riding Hood ate cookies and drank hot cocoa.

HELLO KITTY®

The Little Mermaid

In the deep, blue sea lived a mermaid named Hello Kitty.
She was known throughout the realm for her beautiful singing
voice. She loved her home, but she longed to see life on land.

She had heard stories of the villages on land and was curious about the people who lived there. She imagined what flowers smelled like and how it sounded when birds sang.

Most of all, she wanted to feel the sun.
Sadly, Hello Kitty had to wait until she was a little older
before she could swim to the surface of the sea.

Years passed, until finally Hello Kitty was old enough to swim to the surface. The sky was radiant, and the waves glistened like jewels.

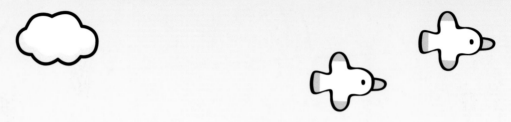

She swam close to the shore, where pink sea roses grew.
She could smell their sweet scent even from the water.

When evening came, Hello Kitty pulled herself onto a rock so she could see all around her. Off in the distance, she heard music and saw a ship covered in lights. It was a birthday celebration for a prince!

The lights and music were so beautiful, and the prince was so handsome, that Hello Kitty did not notice the dark clouds gathering.

Soon, hard rains fell and strong winds blew.
The wind whipped the waves around the prince's boat. The boat
rocked so hard, the prince was thrown overboard.

Hello Kitty dove until she found the prince. With the help
of her dolphin friend, she carried him back to the shore.

Hello Kitty could not stop thinking about the prince.
She spent her days and nights singing sad, beautiful songs.

Finally, Hello Kitty asked the Sea Witch for help. The Sea Witch offered Hello Kitty a potion, but it came with a warning.

If Hello Kitty drank the potion, it would turn her mermaid tail into legs. She'd be able to walk on land and be with the prince. But she would also lose her voice. If the prince didn't fall in love with her, Hello Kitty would lose her voice forever.

Hello Kitty thought long and hard. If she couldn't talk, how could she get to know the prince? But if she couldn't walk, she might never see the prince again!

Hello Kitty decided to take a chance. She swam
to the surface and drank the potion.
She felt her mermaid tail change into two legs.

She walked out of the water and across the sand to the prince's castle.

The prince was hosting a ball that night. Hello Kitty arrived
just in time to dance with the prince. As they danced, the prince
asked Hello Kitty her name. She could not answer.

Suddenly, the prince recognized Hello Kitty!
She was the one who had rescued him when he
fell into the sea!

To show his gratitude, the prince kissed Hello Kitty's cheek. Hello Kitty's voice returned! She sang the prince and his guests the most beautiful song and everyone was very happy.

HELLO KITTY®
The Nutcracker &
The Mouse King

In the heart of winter, when
the wind was high and the
snow was deep,
Grandpa worked in his
cozy workshop.

Upstairs by the fire, Hello
Kitty and her friends could
hear the buzz of the saw
and the hammering of nails.

At last, Grandpa was finished! He invited Hello Kitty and her friends to see what he had been working on.

They could hardly
believe their eyes.
Grandpa's shelves were
filled with the most
magical toys!

To Hello Kitty, the most magical toy of all was a wooden nutcracker hidden on a high shelf.

134

Seeing how much Hello Kitty loved the nutcracker, Grandpa gave her the toy, but first she had to promise to take very good care of it.

135

Overjoyed, Hello Kitty showed her new treasure
to all of her friends. They each wanted
a turn playing with the toy.

Suddenly, CRACK!

Hello Kitty
wrapped the
nutcracker's
broken arm with
one of her ribbons.
Then she cradled
him in her arms.

138

Grandpa took the toy and placed it
back on the high shelf.

At last, it was time for bed. Hello Kitty and her friends changed into their pajamas and Mama and Papa tucked them in tight.

But Hello Kitty couldn't sleep. She couldn't stop thinking about the nutcracker.

While everyone slept, Hello Kitty snuck down to
Grandpa's workshop.

There was something magical about being in Grandpa's workshop when everything was so quiet. Hello Kitty gazed at the nutcracker until she nodded off to sleep.

When the clock struck midnight, Hello Kitty woke with a start. As she watched, a mouse scurried from behind the wall.

He rushed to a wooden music box sitting on a high shelf right next to the nutcracker. When the mouse lifted the lid, the music box played the most beautiful music. The ballerina inside twirled and twirled.

Suddenly, all of the toys on the shelves began to move!

Before Hello Kitty's eyes, they tumbled to the floor one by one. The nutcracker stayed on his shelf, not moving.

147

Hello Kitty brought the nutcracker down carefully and held him in her arms. As the other toys played around her, she whispered to the nutcracker that Grandpa would fix him good as new.

Then she kissed his cheek and
put him back on the shelf.

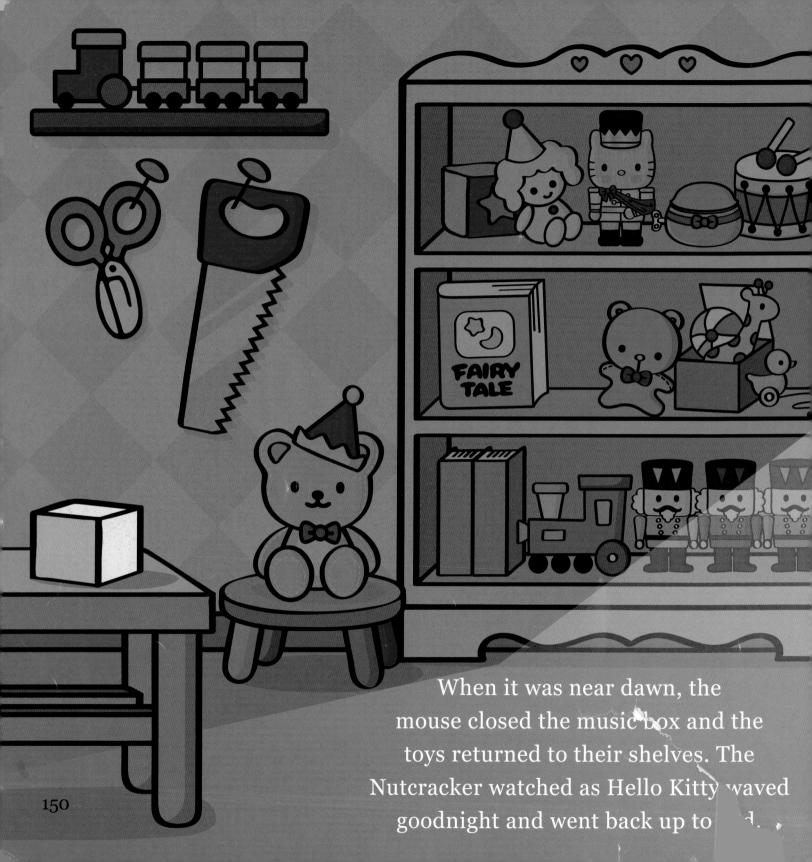

When it was near dawn, the mouse closed the music box and the toys returned to their shelves. The Nutcracker watched as Hello Kitty waved goodnight and went back up to ...d.

The next morning, Hello Kitty told her family and friends
what had happened the night before.

Everyone laughed! She must have
been dreaming! But Grandpa
didn't laugh. He looked at
Hello Kitty and smiled.

The next night, after everyone had gone to sleep, Hello Kitty snuck down to Grandpa's workshop. As before, when the clock struck midnight, the mouse scurried from the wall and opened the music box. As before, the toys came to life.

When Hello Kitty looked
at the nutcracker's shelf,
he wasn't there!

Suddenly, Grandpa walked into the room, holding the nutcracker. His arm wasn't broken anymore!

Grandpa placed the toy in front of Hello Kitty and stood
back. As Hello Kitty watched, the nutcracker grew
until they were the same size. Then he hugged her to
thank her for taking such good care of him.
The toys all cheered!

Hello Kitty's friends came downstairs to see what all the excitement was about.

When they saw that Grandpa's workshop really *had* come to life, they could hardly believe it! They joined in the celebration and marveled at the magic of that cold winter's night.

158

Library of Congress Control Number 2017960629

ISBN 978-1-4197-3215-7

SANRIO®, HELLO KITTY®, and associated logos are trademarks and/or
registered trademarks of Sanrio Co., Ltd.

Text and original art copyright ©1976, 2018 SANRIO CO., LTD.
Graphics and illustrations by Susanne Chambers and Karla A. Alfonzo
Book design by Mercedes Padró

Published in 2018 by Abrams Books for Young Readers,
an imprint of ABRAMS. All rights reserved. No portion of this book may
be reproduced, stored in a retrieval system, or transmitted in any form or by any
means, mechanical, electronic, photocopying, recording, or otherwise,
without written permission from the publisher.

Printed and bound in China
10 9 8 7 6 5 4 3 2 1

Abrams Books for Young Readers are available at special discounts when
purchased in quantity for premiums and promotions as well as fundraising
or educational use. Special editions can also be created to specification. For
details, contact specialsales@abramsbooks.com or the address below.

ABRAMS The Art of Books
195 Broadway, New York, NY 10007
abramsbooks.com